D1573033

Madeleine's Light

A Story of Camille Claudel

Natalie Ziarnik

Illustrated by Robert Dunn

BOYDS MILLS PRESS

To my teachers—past, present, and future

—NZ

For Miss Emily Gwynneth Dunn and Master Caius (the un-sleeping)

—RD

Text copyright © 2012 by Natalie Ziarnik
Illustrations copyright © 2012 by Robert Dunn
All rights reserved

For information about permission to reproduce selections from this book,
please contact permissions@highlights.com.

Photos, p. 32: Camille Claudel by César (1884), from Wikimedia Commons, public
domain; Camille Claudel's *La Petite Châtelaine*, copyright © 2010 by Theresia Winkler,
Winkler Images.

Boyds Mills Press, Inc.
815 Church Street
Honesdale, Pennsylvania 18431
Printed in China

ISBN: 978-1-59078-855-4
Library of Congress Control Number: 2011940124

The text of this book is set in Diotima Light.
The illustrations are done in pencil and watercolor.

10 9 8 7 6 5 4 3 2 1

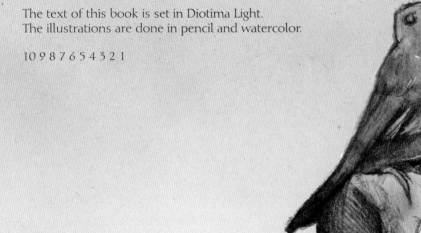

French-English Glossary

au revoir (oh reh-*vwahr*): good-bye

bonjour (bohn-*zhur*): hello; good morning

café au lait (kah-fay oh *lay*): coffee with milk

C'est moi (seh *mwah*): It's me.

C'est toi (seh *twah*): It's you.

château (shah-*toh*): a large country house

grand-mère (grahn-*mair*): grandmother

la lumière (lah lew-me-*air*): the light

ma chérie (mah shey-*ree*): my dear

ma petite (mah puh-*teet*): my little one

non (nohn): no

oui (wee): yes

vite (veet): quick

CENTRAL ARKANSAS LIBRARY SYSTEM
ADOLPHINE FLETCHER TERRY BRANCH
LITTLE ROCK, ARKANSAS

"Grand-mère!" Madeleine shouted.
"The carriage is coming!"

All morning, Madeleine had been waiting for
the guest to arrive at the château.

A team of horses stopped near the front door,
and a tattered black coat and black umbrella
stepped from the carriage. The coat turned around,
and Mademoiselle Claudel's hair swept back to
reveal her violet eyes.

"Vite! Vite!" the young woman growled at a servant as she ordered him to carry boxes of stone and marble figures into the house. Without a word, she walked past Madeleine and Grand-mère and followed the servant to the guest room.

"Is she wild?" Madeleine whispered.

"Just spirited," answered Grand-mère. "It is rare that a woman becomes a talented sculptor."

Over the next few days, Madeleine followed Mademoiselle Claudel.

When the guest-room door was open, Madeleine looked in, but whirls of dust clouded her view.

When the door was closed, she heard objects falling and splintering like shocks of lightning.

One day, Madeleine brought a bowl of *café au lait* to the
artist's room. She saw Mademoiselle Claudel sitting in the dark,
hunched over a table of broken sculptures.

"*Bonjour*, Mademoiselle Claudel," she said, placing the tray on
the table.

Suddenly, the artist stood up. "*La lumière*," she said.

Madeleine opened the shutters to let light—*lumière*—into
the room.

"Not that light," the sculptor said. "I mean the light inside you."
She circled and observed Madeleine from every angle. "A light
of becoming," she said. "*Ma petite*, what are you becoming?"

Madeleine didn't know how to answer the artist and
ran from the room

Outside, in the maze of hedges, Madeleine took a soft clay bird out of her pocket. She felt a sudden poke in her back. When she turned around, the bird fell from her hands.

"I found you!" Mademoiselle Claudel said, her eyes now playful. Then she saw the lump of clay lying on the ground.

"So, ma petite," the artist said, picking up the clay now covered in grass. "You are becoming a sculptor." Mademoiselle Claudel handed the clay back to Madeleine.

"I was making a bird for Grand-mère's birthday," Madeleine said. "Will you help me?"

"*Oui*, ma petite. Tomorrow, we will begin."

The next morning, the two artists wandered in the rain to look for clay. When they came to a stream, they removed their shoes and stockings. Cool mud slid between their toes. They pulled handfuls of red, rich clay, gathered it in their skirts, and walked home.

"What if Grand-mère sees us covered in mud?" asked Madeleine.

"No matter," the sculptor said, holding the earth close to her heart. "This clay glows with life."

Layer by layer, Mademoiselle Claudel and Madeleine
shaped the clay, smoothing the rough spots away. Madeleine
formed the belly and head of a bird.

Mademoiselle Claudel sculpted in the corner. Sometimes she
paused and covered her own work with a wet cloth. Then she
showed the young artist how to use sculpting tools to define the
details of the bird's body—its feathered back and delicate eyes.

As Mademoiselle Claudel shaped her own clay, her eyes sparkled and her fingers danced.

"May I see what you are working on?" Madeleine asked one afternoon.

"Ma petite," the sculptor said, again covering her work with a wet cloth, "just as the bird you are making is a surprise for Grand-mère, my work is also a surprise."

A week before Grand-mère's birthday, Madeleine shaped her bird's beak.

She made the beak thinner. But it did not look real.

She made the beak thicker. But the beak still did not look as it should.

"*Non! Non!*" she said, throwing her sculpting tool on the floor. "The bird's beak is not right. Grand-mère will never like it."

"Patience, ma petite," Mademoiselle Claudel said. "Leave your work. Let's go outside."

In the sunshine, the two artists chased butterflies and collected bouquets of lavender. They sat by the pond and listened to the birds.

"That's it!" Madeleine said, watching a bird in a tree. "The bird's beak is open so it can sing."

Madeleine flew back into the house, eager to work.

Finally, Grand-mère's birthday had come.

"Close your eyes, Grand-mère," Madeleine said. "Make a nest with your hands."

Madeleine placed the finished bird—painted and fired—in her grandmother's palms.

Grand-mère's fingers explored the shape and texture of the little statue, and then she opened her eyes to see the sculpted bird. She gave Madeleine a hug.

"*Ma chérie*, you have become a sculptor!" Grand-mère smiled.

"Now I have something to show you," said Mademoiselle Claudel.

The sculptor led them upstairs to her room and removed the wet cloth from her work.

Grand-mère gasped.

Madeleine studied the bust up close. *"C'est moi?"* she asked.

"Oui, c'est toi," Mademoiselle Claudel answered. "Your light captured my heart."

Early the next morning, dressed in her old black coat, Mademoiselle Claudel climbed into her carriage. The bust of Madeleine sat beside her.

"*Au revoir*!" said Madeleine.

"Wait! I almost forgot," said Mademoiselle Claudel.

"This is for you. Au revoir, ma petite."

About the Story

Camille Claudel (1864–1943) was a noted French sculptor at a time when few women pursued the arts professionally. As a child, she showed an early talent for sculpture and later moved to Paris, where she studied and worked with Auguste Rodin while developing her own lyrical style.

Madeleine's Light is a fictional story of a period in Claudel's life. During the summers of 1890–1893, Claudel stayed at the Château de l'Islette to work in peace, away from the chaos and art critics of Paris. She became friends with the landlady's granddaughter, Madeleine Boyer. In many ways, Claudel saw Madeleine as a younger version of herself.

Madeleine was such an inspiration to Claudel that she created several versions of the bust based on her image. One of these is named *Young Joan of Arc* and shows the passion of the French heroine as she may have appeared at an early age. Another version, *La Petite Châtelaine (The Little Lady)*, can be seen today at the Musée Rodin in Paris. This work is seen as a turning point in Claudel's artistic life, the point at which she sought to capture more than the outlines of a person's face; she hoped to depict the person's soul and individual character as well.

Very little is known about Madeleine Boyer or what happened to her later in life. In this story, she portrays many of the characteristics that were typical of Claudel when she was a young girl and artist: a passionate temperament, a curious mind, a connection to nature, a yearning toward excellence in her art, and an ability to concentrate with the hands as well as the mind.

Sources

Ayral-Clause, Odile. *Camille Claudel: A Life*. New York: Harry N. Abrams, 2002.

Caranfa, Angelo. *Camille Claudel: A Sculpture of Interior Solitude*. Lewisburg, PA: Bucknell University Press, 1999.

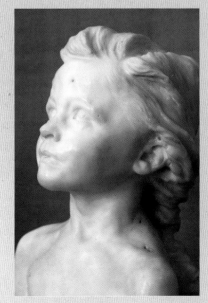

La Petite Châtelaine